Maggie + me

by paula

For Finnley True
I love you
forever

DIAL BOOKS FOR YOUNG READERS • Penguin Young Readers Group

An imprint of Penguin Random House LLC • 375 Hudson Street, New York, New York 10014

Copyright © 2016 by Hannah E. Harrison

Library of Congress Cataloging-in-Publication Data • Harrison, Hannah E., author, illustrator.

My friend Maggie / Hannah E. Harrison. • pages cm

Summary: "Paula and Maggie are best friends until Paula starts playing with some new friends instead, but when her new playmates turn on her, it's Maggie who rushes to Paula's defense"— Provided by publisher. • ISBN 978-0-525-42916-6 (hardcover)

[1. Best friends—Fiction. 2. Friendship—Fiction.] i. Title. • PZ7.H2488My 2016 [E]—dc23 2015018462

Manufactured in China on acid-free paper • 10 9 8 7 6 5 4 3 2 1

Designed by Jason Henry • Text set in Klepto ITC • The artwork for this book was created with acrylic paint on Bristol board . . . except for Paula's drawing, which was created with colored pencil by Lila Quinn Harrison.

My Friend Maggie

Hannah E.
Harrison

DIAL BOOKS FOR YOUNG READERS

This is my friend Maggie.

Maggie

EVERGREEN
ELEMENTARY

Me!
(Paula)

We've been friends forever.

She's great at splashing in mud puddles.

She helps me reach the reddest apples.

She even lifts me up when I can't see.

Maggie's the best!

Only . . . Veronica
doesn't think so.

Veronica thinks Maggie's too big.
And now that she mentions it . . .

Maggie *is* kind of clumsy.

She *stinks* at hide-and-seek.

And her clothes *are* a little snuggish.

I know I should stick up
for Maggie . . .

. . . but I play with Veronica instead.

And I pretend I don't see Maggie

(even though she's impossible to miss).

But then Veronica decides that my teeth stick out too far and starts calling me Bucky.

And do you know who comes
charging in to stand up for me?

Maggie!

Can you believe it?

Yup.
This is my friend Maggie!

Did I mention
she's the best?

I'll be her friend forever.